W9-AUC-311

JULIA DONALDSON

ILLUSTRATED BY
LYDIA MONKS

WHAT THE LADYBUG HEARD AT THE ZOO

Henry Holt and Company · New York

One fine day when the sun shone down,
The ladybug took a trip to town.
She flew around and she saw the sights—
The streets and the shops and the bright, bright lights.
She saw the parks, and the palace, too,
Then off she flew to visit the zoo.

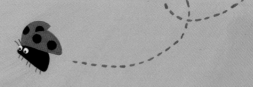

In memory of Willow and Holly,
the Queen's corgis

Henry Holt and Company, *Publishers since 1866*
Henry Holt® is a registered trademark of Macmillan Publishing Group, LLC
175 Fifth Avenue, New York, NY 10010 • mackids.com

Text copyright © 2017 by Julia Donaldson
Illustrations copyright © 2017 by Lydia Monks
All rights reserved.

Library of Congress Cataloging-in-Publication Data
Names: Donaldson, Julia, author. | Monks, Lydia, illustrator.
Title: What the ladybug heard at the zoo / Julia Donaldson ; illustrated by Lydia Monk.
Description: First American edition. | New York : Henry Holt and Company, 2019. | "Originally published in the United Kingdom in 2017 by Macmillan Children's Books."
Summary: The ladybug goes to town and visits a zoo, where she overhears Hefty Hugh and Lanky Len plotting to take a monkey and use him to rob the queen.
Identifiers: LCCN 2018038718 | ISBN 978-1-250-15670-9 (hardcover)
Subjects: | CYAC: Stories in rhyme. | Ladybugs—Fiction. | Zoo animals—Fiction. | Zoos—Fiction. | Robbers and outlaws—Fiction.
Classification: LCC PZ8.3.D7235 Whd 2019 | DDC [E]—dc23
LC record available at https://lccn.loc.gov/2018038718

Our books may be purchased in bulk for promotional, educational, or business use. Please contact your local bookseller or the
Macmillan Corporate and Premium Sales Department at (800) 221-7945 ext. 5442 or by email at MacmillanSpecialMarkets@macmillan.com.

Originally published in the United Kingdom in 2017 by Macmillan Children's Books
First American edition, 2019
Printed in China by Shenzhen Wing King Tong Paper Products Co. Ltd., Shenzhen City, Guangdong Province

1 3 5 7 9 10 8 6 4 2

But the ladybug never said a word.

Then the crocodile grinned, and the tiger pranced,
The lion leaped and the monkeys danced,
The elephant trumpeted—*trump, trump, trump!*
"Hooray!" said the camel with the great big hump.
The hyena laughed and the hummingbird whirred,

The thieves took off with leaps and bounds,
Pursued by all the hungry hounds,
While the monkey ran and the ladybug flew
With never a stop till they reached the zoo.

They seized the bones, and gnashed and gnawed,
Tugged and tussled, pawed and clawed,
Then turned upon the robbers, yelping,
"How about a second helping?"

A poodle and a Labrador,
A Peke, a pug, then more and more.
Black dogs, white dogs, gray and brown—
It seemed like every dog in town.

Just then, a dog came bounding up,
And Hugh said, "Shoo, you greedy pup!"
Another dog was close behind,
And then came dogs of every kind.

Corgi Holly and Corgi Willow,
Who lay on each side of the Queen's soft pillow,
Were wide awake, and they said to Joe,
"Come on, Monkey—off we go."

Then they rubbed their hands as they saw him creeping
Into the room where the Queen lay sleeping.

You should have heard their moans and groans
To find the sack was full of bones!

The two thieves yelled, "Hip hip hooray!
But now let's make our getaway."

They carried the sack to a nice, quiet park
Where the only sound was a distant bark.
They found a bench and both sat down,
And Hugh said, "Time to see that crown!"
"I just can't wait," said Lanky Len.
They opened up the sack, but then . . .

They led the way while the Queen still slept,
And they showed young Joe where their bones were kept.
Then they helped the monkey fill the sack,
And they wagged their tails as he carried it back.

They carried him off to the palace gate,
Gave him a sack, then lay in wait.
They watched him scale the palace wall,
And they muttered, "Careful not to fall!"

At dead of night the two bad men,
Hefty Hugh and Lanky Len,
Checked there was no one else about,
Then they picked the lock and they got Joe out.

And both the dogs agreed to do
Just what the ladybug told them to.

Then fast as the wind, fast as a bird,
She flew to the palace, and had a word
With the Queen's two corgis, Willow and Holly,
And one said, "Gosh!" and the other said, "Golly!"

But the ladybug told them not to fear,
And she whispered a plan in the monkey's ear.

The little ladybug spread the word
About the plan that she'd overheard.

And the crocodile snapped, and the tiger growled,
The lion roared and the monkeys howled,
The elephant trumpeted—*trump, trump, trump!*
"Humph," said the camel with the great big hump.
The hyena cried and the hummingbird whirred,
And all of the animals, feathered and furred,
Said, "No no no! NO NO NO!
We can't let them kidnap Monkey Joe!"

He'll find out where the Queen's asleep,
Then—*tiptoe*—into her room he'll creep.
He'll open the sack and steal the crown.
We'll soon be the richest men in town!"

"We'll hide till there's no one else about,
Then we'll pick the lock and we'll get Joe out,
And if we give him lots of fruit
He'll do the job and he'll get the loot.
The palace isn't far at all.
Monkey Joe can scale the wall.

She saw two men she already knew.
They were Lanky Len and Hefty Hugh,
And she heard them chuckle, "Ho ho ho!
We're going to kidnap Monkey Joe."

But the ladybug saw, and the ladybug heard . . .

The elephant trumpeted—
trump, trump, trump!

"Humph," said the camel
with the great big hump.

The hyena laughed and
the hummingbird whirred,

But the ladybug
never said a word.

And the crocodile snapped,
and the tiger growled,

The lion roared
and the monkeys howled,

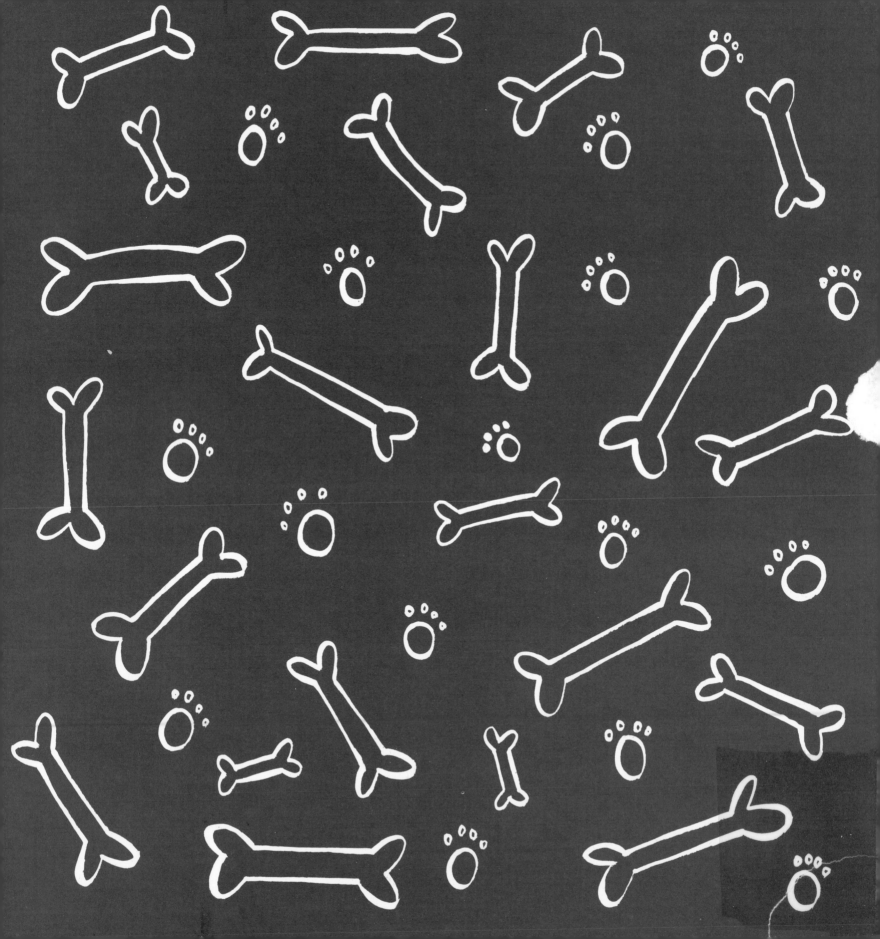